Best wishes,

Lisa Funari-Willever

Chumpkin

Special Guest Young Author & Illustrator Section

Lisa Funari Willever & Lorraine Funari

Illustrated by
Emma Overman

Franklin Mason Press

Trenton, New Jersey

This book is dedicated to Anjuli Jacobs.

For my father-in-law, Cliff and his beautiful pumpkin patch, the best I've ever seen.
Also, for Richard, Cliff, Nick, Scott, Samantha, Daniel, Salvatore, Cody and Ryan...**LFW**
To Jessica and Patrick, my two little loves...**LF**
For anyone who's ever been picked last...**EO**

The editors at Franklin Mason Press would like to offer their gratitude to those who have contributed their time and energy to this project: Ms. Rebecca Matthias, Mr. Dan Matthias, Mr. Reynold Funari, Mr. Priit Pals, Ms. Karen Pals, Mr. Donald Greenwood, Mr. Robert Quackenbush, Mr. Jim Overman, Ms. Mary Ann Overman, Ms. Karen Aiello, Ms. Geraldine Willever, Ms. Patti Willever, Mr. Brian Hughes, Ms. Adrienne Supino, Ms. Wanda Bowman, Ms. Nancy Volpe, Ms. Stacey Williams, Ms. Dawn Hiltner and all of our friends at the New Jersey Education Association and the National Education Association.

Also, a special thanks to those who have worked on the Guest Young Author & Illustrator Committees. Your care in selecting the work of young authors and artists will help to shape and inspire the writers and illustrators of tomorrow.

the four foundation

Franklin Mason Press is proud to support the important work of The Four Foundation. In that spirit, $0.25 will be donated from the sale of each book. To learn more about their work, visit their site at www.fourfoundation.org.

All around the pumpkin patch, they heard the farmer say:

"The kids are here! The kids are here!
It's time for Pumpkin Day!"

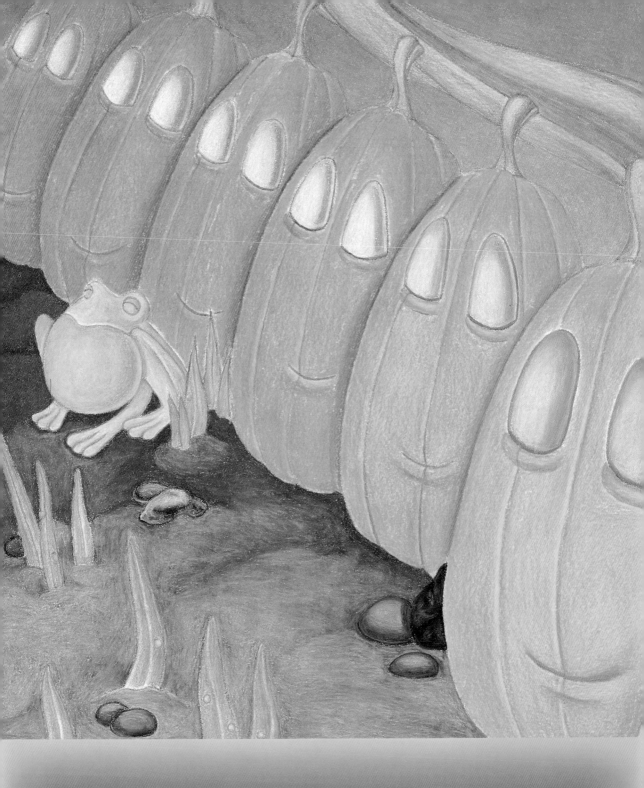

Excited little pumpkins
were standing straight and tall...

that is, except for Chumpkin,
the roundest one of all.

Pumpkins may be orange,
but Chumpkin, he felt blue.

And how he wished that he could shrink,
but every day he grew!

Now, rumbling up the driveway and
stopping at the gate...

L BUS

were giant yellow buses filled,
with kids who couldn't wait.

Jumping from the buses,
the sounds of little feet.
Running to the pumpkin patch,
to find an orange treat.

A day of pumpkin picking
in the cool October air,
Chumpkin dreamt of being chosen,
but pretended not to care.

"I know they'll never pick me,"
he mumbled with a sigh.
"Unless they plan to use me
in a giant pumpkin pie!"

"For no one wants a pumpkin
that grows bigger every day.
What will the other pumpkins think?
What will the others say?"

"I wish these kids would just go home!"
Chumpkin raved and ranted.
"I think it would be better
if I never had been planted."

"If only they would put me on
a fat-free pumpkin diet.
I'd finally hear those magic words,
"Hey, Mister can I buy it?"

"One by one, they're bringing home
my little pumpkin friends.
But no one even looks my way
could this be how it ends?"

"I'll be the only pumpkin,
in a patch of wild weeds.
Maybe then they'll want me when
they need some pumpkin seeds."

But Pumpkin Day was over
and soon it would be night.

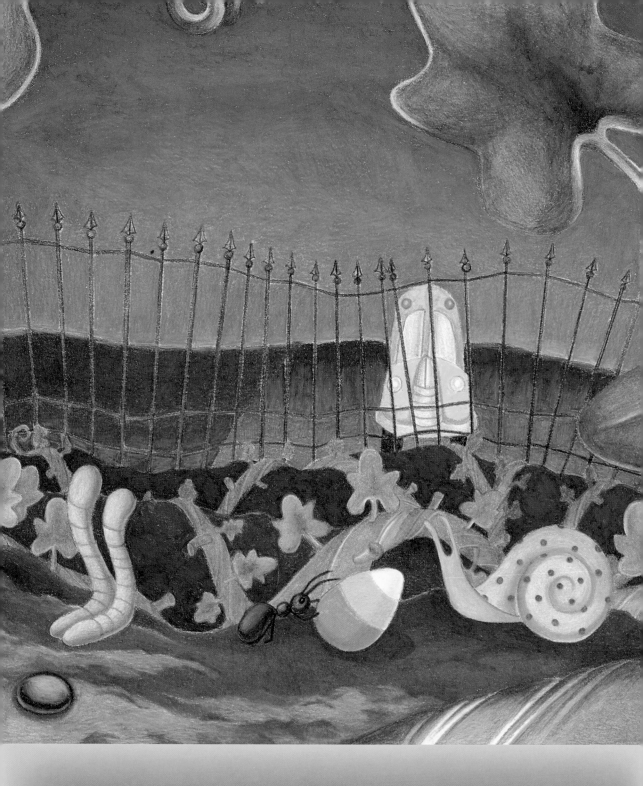

As squealing little children left,
with everything in sight.

Except for poor ol' Chumpkin,
who was doing less than fine.

The last one in the pumpkin patch,
the last one on the vine.

Then suddenly ... some footsteps
and Chumpkin heard, "SURPRISE!"

As the farmer told his little son
to open up his eyes.

And when he opened up his eyes
he started hugging Chumpkin-
"Daddy, can I have him?
Can I have the biggest pumpkin?"

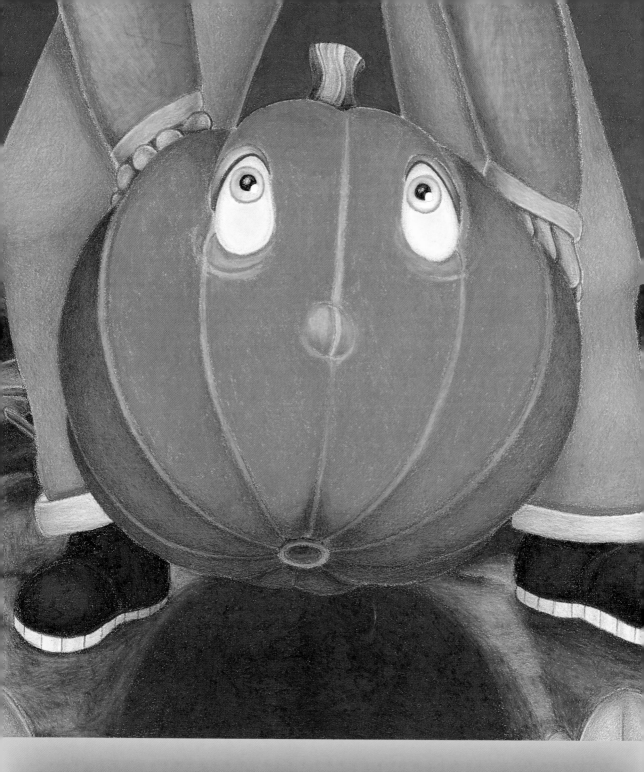

"Of course, you can!" the farmer said.
"I've saved him just for you!
We'll make a jack-o'-lantern.
You can help me carve him, too!"

"But I would never carve a pumpkin,
with a face as nice as his.
I think my pumpkin's perfect,
Daddy, just the way he is!"

Guest Young Author

 1st

Katie Foley—Age 8

Roosevelt Elementary School

River Edge, New Jersey

"A Poem About Books"

Down I go, flop on my bed,

First on my belly, then on my head.

Goblins, fairies, animals, too.

Giants, reindeer, and a pig that is blue.

I get so involved, I can't turn out the light.

11:59! Oh my gosh, it's midnight!

A book about June is a book that I like.

Sometimes she plays football: hut, hut, hike!

There's a house on a prairie, it's my favorite book.

Right next to the house is a cool little brook.

A funny cat story is the first that I read,

Man, I think I'm getting ahead!

I loved a book about the moon and a book about a bunny,

But now, I think all those books are funny.

Books, books, they're fun to read.

If I have a book, it's all I need.

2nd

Catherine Makoski—Age 8

Sayen Elementary School

Hamilton, New Jersey

"My Pet Sylvester"

3rd

Jerhud Buhagiar—Age 9

Hull Elementary School

Livonia, Michigan

"The Dragon and The Mouse"

Guest Young Illustrator

 1st

Christopher Saxton—Age 8

Sunnybrae Elementary School—Hamilton, New Jersey

"When I Move Into The White House"

 2nd

Girija Hariharan—Age 6

Mawbey Street School

Woodbridge, New Jersey

"My Favorite Place"

 3rd

Ava Howland—Age 7

Pen Ryn School

Levittown, Pennsylvania

"The Lone Wolf"

Would You Like To Be An Author or Illustrator?

Franklin Mason Press is looking for stories and illustrations from children 6-9 years old to appear in our books. We are dedicated to providing children with an avenue into the world of publishing. If you would like to be our next Guest Young Author or Guest Young Illustrator, read the information below and send us your work.

To be a Guest Young Author: Send us a 75-200 word story about something strange, funny, or unusual. Stories may be fiction or non-fiction. Be sure to follow the rules below.

To be a Guest Young Illustrator: Draw a picture using crayons, markers, or colored pencils. Do not write words on your picture and be sure to follow the rules below.

Prizes

1st Place Author / 1st Place Illustrator
$25.00, a framed award, a complimentary book and your work will be published in FMP's newest book.

2nd Place Author / 2nd Place Illustrator
$15.00, a framed award, a complimentary book and the title of your work and your name will be published in FMP's newest book.

3rd Place Author / 3rd Place Illustrator
$10.00, a framed award, a complimentary book and the title of your work and your name will be published in FMP's newest book.

Rules For The Contest

1. Children may enter one category only, either Author or Illustrator.
2. All stories must be typed or written very neatly.
3. All illustrations must be sent in between 2 pieces of cardboard to prevent wrinkling.
4. Name, address, phone number, school, and parent's signature must be on the back of all submissions.
5. All work must be original and completed solely by the child.
6. Franklin Mason Press reserves the right to print submitted material. All work becomes property of FMP and will not be returned. Any work selected is considered a work for hire and FMP will retain all rights.
7. There is no deadline for submissions. FMP will publish children's work in every book published. All submissions are considered for the most current title.
8. All submissions should be sent to: Youth Submissions Editor, Franklin Mason Press, P.O. Box 3808, Trenton, NJ 08629, **www.franklinmason.com**

About The Four Foundation

the four foundation

Franklin Mason Press is proud to donate twenty-five cents, from the sale of each copy of Chumpkin sold, to the Four Foundation. Below, we have provided information about their valuable work in the area of pediatric brain tumors. We are honored to play a role in their important mission.

The Four Foundation was founded for the purpose of assisting researchers at Columbia-Presbyterian Medical Center in developing new and successful treatments for children stricken with brain tumors, as well as to increase the cure rate for these children and to spare them and their parents the anguish of such a horrible illness. Current treatments allow only for the medicine and technology of the past. Treatment of brain tumors has not substantially advanced in decades. Only with research can there be hope for the future. Only with research can children have a fighting chance to overcome their brain tumors with complete confidence.

The Four Foundation's driving commitment is fueled with desire and pledged to, "Whoever saves one life, saves the world entire."

Four Foundation — 173 Pascack Avenue, Emerson, NJ 07630 — 201-265-8440   tarallo@fourfoundation.org

Commendable Acts of Humanity by Children

The editors of Franklin Mason Press are always impressed by the wonderful things accomplished by children. In addition to honoring our Guest Young Authors and Illustrators, we would like to commend the following children for their extraordinary demonstrations of humanity.

INDIVIDUAL — William Blanche, Bobby Bostock, George Delvalle, Ed Renolds, and Gloria Soc

SMALL GROUP CATEGORY (Groups of 2-10 persons) —
Hedgepath/Williams Middle School - Peer Mediators, Yardville Heights EarlyAct Club

CLASSROOM (Groups of more than 10 persons) —
Franklin Elementary School, Mrs. Graham's 3rd Grade, Sacred Heart Elementary School, Mrs. Nitti's 3rd Grade, Immaculate Conception Elementary School Red Cross Club

Their good deeds and selflessness are not only an example for other children, but for young and old alike. If you would like to nominate a child for their acts of kindness or humanity, please visit our website or send a letter to Franklin Mason Press, Youth Submissions Editor, P.O. Box 3808, Trenton, NJ 08629

About the Authors & Illustrator

Lisa Funari Willever (author) is a lifelong resident of Trenton, New Jersey and a fourth grade teacher in the Trenton School District. She is a graduate of The College of New Jersey and a member of the National Education Association, the New Jersey Education Association, and the New Jersey Reading Association. She is also the author of The Culprit Was A Fly, Miracle On Theodore's Street, Maximilian The Great, The Easter Chicken, and Everybody Moos At Cows. Her husband, Todd is a professional Firefighter in the city of Trenton and the co-author of Miracle of Theodore's Street. They are the proud parents of two year old Jessica and one year old Patrick.

Lorraine Funari (author) is a lifelong resident of Mercer County, New Jersey and the mother of three grown children, Lisa, Anthony, and Paula. Her husband, Reynold, is a meat cutter in Hamilton, New Jersey. She is also the co-author of Maximilian The Great and The Easter Chicken.

Emma Overman (illustrator) is a freelance illustrator and muralist. She received her Bachelor of Arts from Hanover College in Indiana and completed a Post Baccalaureate Program at Maryland Institute College of Art. Born in Brazil and raised in Tennessee, Emma now resides in Indianapolis, Indiana. She has also illustrated The Easter Chicken.

About Franklin Mason Press Franklin Mason Press was founded in Trenton, New Jersey in September 1999. While our main goal is to produce quality reading materials, we also provide children with an avenue into the world of publishing. Our Guest Young Author and Illustrator Contest offers children an opportunity to submit their work and possibly become published authors and illustrators. In addition, Franklin Mason Press is proud to support children's charities with donations from book sales. Each new title benefits a different children's charity. For more information please visit our website at: www.franklinmason.com

Franklin Mason Press

P.O. Box 3808, Trenton, NJ 08629